CASEBUSTERS

Fear Stalks Grizzly Hill

Disney Adventures

CASEBUSTERS

⑨

Fear Stalks Grizzly Hill

By Joan Lowery Nixon

Disney PRESS

New York

To my talented daughter, Kathy, with my love—J. L. N.

Library of Congress Catalog Card Number: 96-85364
ISBN: 0-7868-4086-2 (pbk.)

1

SEAN QUINN PEERED out of the car at the dense tangle of trees and bushes that lined the road, half-hoping to see a bear. He shivered as he wondered what would happen if a bear spotted *him* instead. His parents' friends had recently moved to a house on Grizzly Hill, and Sean was beginning to think that it wasn't such a good idea that he and Brian were about to spend the weekend with them.

Sean turned to Mr. and Mrs. Nash's son and asked, "Alan, have you ever seen any grizzly bears in the woods?"

Alan looked puzzled. "There aren't any grizzly bears around here."

"Then why'd they name this place Grizzly Hill?"

Mrs. Nash turned from the front seat and smiled. "Long, long ago—more than one hundred years ago—a giant grizzly was supposed to have lived in a den in the area."

"Was there really a den?"

"Yes. And it's still there. Alan knows where it is. You boys can crawl in and explore the cave if you'd like."

Sean's heart gave a jump. "Is the giant bear still around?" he whispered.

"Bears don't live to be that old," Brian told him.

"But there could be other bears," Sean insisted.

Mrs. Nash explained, "Sean, the developer of this subdivision called it Grizzly Hill because he liked the name. Trust me. There are no bears around here."

Mr. Nash turned off the highway onto a road that wound up a steep hill. The forest on either side looked dark and scary. At the moment Sean wished that his parents hadn't both gone out of town on business at the same time.

Bri had complained about Mom hiring Mrs. Peabody to take care of them. "We're too old for sitters," he'd insisted, "and it would be a lot of fun to stay with the Nashes in their new home. Alan said they find all sorts of animal tracks around their house. I can bring plaster of paris and make casts for my science project. Please, Mom? Sean and I want to stay with the Nashes."

Sean wished now that he'd told Mom he wanted Mrs. Peabody. He'd rather deal with her than with a bear.

The road swept up to a wide clearing in the forest. Facing the circular road were five large, beautiful homes.

"Wow!" Sean said.

"Cool!" Brian said.

"So far, these are the only houses that have been built in Grizzly Hill," Mr. Nash told them.

He began to point out a spot off to the left where another road would soon be constructed, with more houses and neighbors, but Sean didn't listen. As he climbed from the car he was aware of the forest pressing in around them, and he didn't like it at all.

The Nash house was in the center, with two houses on each side. There were no neighbors in sight, although Brian saw a curtain move in a window of the tall colonial house on the far right.

Apparently Alan did, too, because he nudged Brian and said, "Mr. and Mrs. Webber live there. Mrs. Webber always wants to see what's going on." He waved, and the curtain quickly dropped.

Mr. and Mrs. Nash led them into their home. "You two are in the guest bedroom upstairs, and you can put your knapsacks there. Alan will show you the way," Mr. Nash said.

But Mrs. Nash put a hand on Alan's arm to stop him. "Wait. The boys haven't met Lucy," she said.

The girl who came into the entry hall was tall and slender with dark brown hair. "Lucy's sixteen," Alan had told them and made a face. "Big sisters are so bossy."

Lucy smiled when Mrs. Nash introduced Brian and Sean, but as soon as her parents had walked back to the kitchen, Lucy scowled. "There are a few rules around here you'd better learn right away," she said. "You can't use the phone when I need to use it, you can't run around making noise, and anybody who dares to set foot in my room is in big trouble. Got it?"

"Who'd want to be in your dumb old room anyway?" Alan asked.

"Just don't give me any trouble, or you'll be sorry," Lucy said. Before any of them could answer she ran upstairs.

"Big sisters!" Alan said, and rolled his eyes.

As Brian and Sean dumped their knapsacks

in the guest bedroom, Alan said, "It rained yesterday. The ground is soft, so we ought to be able to find a lot of animal and bird tracks."

"Let's go!" Brian said.

They ran down the stairs and out to the backyard. A small patio was ringed with flowers. Beyond was a narrow strip where grass was trying hard to grow in spite of heavy shade from the large oaks and pines.

Brian bent to study the muddy patches where grass was sparse. "Hey, look!" he said. "Crow tracks . . . sparrow . . . and I know that one, too. It's rabbit."

Sean pointed to pawprints under one of the nearby trees. They were short and wide, with long claw marks. "What are those?" he asked.

"I don't know," Brian said.

Alan shrugged. "Me either."

Sean drew in a shaky breath and took a step back from the overhanging trees. "Look at the size of those claws! They're grizzly bear tracks, aren't they?"

"I told you, there aren't any grizzlies around here," Alan said.

"Besides, the paws are too small for a grizzly," Brian added.

"Maybe it's a young grizzly bear," Sean said. He glanced at the strange tracks again and backed even farther away.

"There's one way to find out," Brian said. He pointed to the prints, which led off to the right. "We'll follow the tracks and see what we find."

2

BRIAN RETURNED TO the house to get his plaster of paris. He mixed some of it with water in a large measuring cup with a spout and when he came back outside, he poured the smooth, white liquid into a few of the nearest tracks.

"Those won't take long to dry," he said. "Pretty soon we'll have some casts we can study."

Sean mumbled, "I don't want anything to do with the claw-footed thing that made those tracks." But Brian and Alan began to follow the prints, and Sean didn't want to be left alone, so he hurried to catch up with them.

The tracks wandered up into the grass, then back into the damp earth. The boys followed them into the forest, but the tracks soon turned and left the forest, making clear impressions in the mud. They led to a tall oak with a thick, twisted trunk, just behind the patio of the house next door to the Nash house.

Brian looked carefully around the base of the tree then said, "The tracks stop here. There aren't any leading away from the tree."

Sean stared upward into the tree's wide-spread branches. He was glad that nothing looked back at him. "Grizzly bears climb trees," he said. "I saw it in a movie."

Brian and Alan glanced upward, too. "They don't stay in trees," Brian said. "This animal—whatever it is—went up and didn't come down."

"Unless it flew away," Alan said, and laughed.

"Bears don't fly," Sean said.

"Maybe it swung from tree to tree," Brian teased.

"Yeah? Well, maybe it's hiding up there and is going to jump down and get us," Sean complained.

Brian asked Alan, "You said you'd take us to the giant grizzly's den. How about now?"

"It's too late," Alan answered. "It'll be dark soon. Want to go first thing in the morning?"

"Sure," Brian said.

"No way," Sean said.

Suddenly, something huge and hairy rushed past Sean and jumped on Alan, knocking him into Brian. The container of plaster of paris mix flew out of Brian's hands as he fell.

"Help!" Sean yelled. "Bears! Help!"

"It's okay," Alan said. "It's just Rusty. Down, Rusty! Down! I haven't got any dog yummies with me."

Brian scrambled to his feet. "That's the biggest St. Bernard dog I've ever seen," he said.

"Or else the hairiest," Sean said.

A tall, thin man rushed up and snapped a leash on Rusty. "Sit, Rusty! Sit! Stay!" he yelled.

Rusty paid no attention. He bounced around, jerking the man who clung to the leash.

Alan shook his head. "Rusty only obeys three commands—down, sit, and stay," he told Brian and Sean.

"He isn't obeying them now," Sean said.

The man's face grew red with anger as he

continued to shout at Rusty.

Alan said, "That's Mr. Trent Everitt. He lives in the house on the far left. Rusty only obeys Mr. Everitt when he feels like it, but he obeys when other people tell him to *stay* or *sit*. Mr. Shaw taught those commands to Rusty."

"Who owns Rusty?" Brian asked. "Mr. Shaw or Mr. Everitt?"

"Mr. Everitt," Alan answered. "But he travels a lot, and when he does, Rusty stays with Mr. and Mrs. Shaw."

Rusty finally tired of his game and settled down. Alan introduced Brian and Sean to Mr. Everitt.

Mr. Everitt didn't smile. He glared at Brian and Sean. "I moved to this development after I retired because it was supposed to be *quiet*," he snapped. "You boys are not only making much too much noise and exciting my dog, you're also littering!"

"Littering?" Sean asked in surprise.

With his free hand Mr. Everitt pointed to the upturned bowl and the splatters of plaster of paris.

"I can explain," Brian said. "I'm making plaster casts of some of the animal tracks around here for my science class project. The plaster spilled, but . . ."

Mr. Everitt interrupted. "No excuses," he grumbled. "Just clean up that mess you've made."

Brian picked up one of the first plaster casts. "This one's dry already," he said and held it out. "Look. See the short, wide footpad and the marks from claws?"

Mr. Everitt stopped scowling and stared at

the cast. "Where did you get that?"

"Right here," Brian said. "And I've made casts of more of the tracks in the forest."

"Do you know what kind of animal made those tracks?" Mr. Everitt looked at Brian warily.

"Not yet," Brian said. "Do you?"

Mr. Everitt studied the paw print. "It could be a cat. Glen Webber recently brought home some cats. One of them might have gotten out last night."

Brian shook his head. "It would have to be an awfully big cat to have long claws like these. Have you seen Mr. Webber's cats?"

"No," Mr. Everitt grumbled. "Glen's not the friendliest of neighbors. He keeps pretty much to himself. I've never been inside his house."

"Tomorrow we're going to look for tracks

around the grizzly's den," Alan said. "We may even find the animal that made them."

"Don't count on it," Mr. Everitt snapped. "Go home, where your parents can keep their eyes on you. If you care anything about the safety of animals in the wild and the peace of the people who live here, you'll leave the forest alone."

Tugging on Rusty's leash, he stomped off toward his house.

"Don't pay attention to him," Alan whispered. "Mr. Everitt is always an old crab. Besides, we're not bothering the animals."

Brian studied the plaster cast in his hands. "The animal who made these paw prints isn't large enough to be a grizzly, but the pads on his feet do look something like a bear's."

"I told you!" Sean said, his heart racing.

"That thing we were tracking *is* a bear! And where do bears go? To their dens, that's where. If we crawl into that grizzly's den tomorrow, we're going to find him waiting for us!"

S TOP WORRYING about bears," Brian said. "Help me pick everything up." He scraped up the splatters of plaster and put them into the empty measuring cup. Then he, Sean, and Alan collected the casts of the strange-looking tracks.

Brian examined each one, brushing the dirt from them. "Most of these are good," he said happily. "They'll be great in my report. The only problem is that I'll have to identify them. What animal made the tracks? And where are we going to find it?"

"C'mon," Alan said. "I'm getting hungry. We can take a shortcut home through the Shaws' backyard. They won't care."

Sean looked around and saw that they had traveled in a semicircle through the edge of the forest behind the houses on Grizzly Hill. As they walked across the grass behind a red brick house, Sean glanced at a window.

A large lizard with a hideous dragonlike face peered through the glass at Sean.

"Yikes!" Sean cried out. "What's that thing?"

"A pet iguana," Alan said.

"It's more like a pet monster," Sean said. "Who'd want to snuggle up with a pet like that? Dracula? Frankenstein?"

"Mr. and Mrs. Arthur Shaw," Alan said. He lowered his voice as a short, heavyset man walked around the corner of his house and came toward them. "Here comes Mr. Shaw now."

Mr. Shaw greeted Alan with a smile, and shook hands as Brian and Sean were introduced. He nodded toward the plaster casts in Brian's hands and asked, "What have you got there?"

"Casts I made of some weird paw prints we found among the trees," Brian said. He handed him the cast on top. "See the marks from the long claws? We don't know what animal this is."

Mr. Shaw shook his head. "I'm afraid I can't help you," he said. But he studied the cast with such concern that Brian wondered if the print meant something to Mr. Shaw—something he wasn't telling.

"Do you know what—?" Brian began, but Mr. Shaw interrupted.

"I think you'd better ask someone else," he said.

"Tomorrow morning we're going exploring in the woods," Alan told him, "so maybe we'll see the animal and find out. I'm going to show Brian and Sean the giant grizzly's den."

Mr. Shaw looked stern as he said, "Under the circumstances, it might be better if you stayed out of the woods."

"Why?" Alan asked.

Mr. Shaw fumbled for an answer. Finally, he said, "Well, we aren't sure what kind of animal this is, are we? It could be dangerous."

"Are we talking about *bears*?" Sean asked.

For an instant Mr. Shaw looked startled, "What's all this about bears?" he asked.

"Don't mind Sean. He's worried about meeting up with a grizzly," Brian said. He took the plaster cast back from Mr. Shaw as he said, "Do you know a lot about animals?"

"I do have an interesting collection of pets," Mr. Shaw said. "My wife and I care for a pair of parakeets, some tropical fish, and the iguana, which lives in a glass aquarium on a table by the large window."

"How'd you happen to get an iguana?" Sean asked.

"Someone brought him to the local animal shelter. She didn't want him. No one wanted him. I felt sorry for the poor little thing, so I brought him home with me. Since my retirement I've been spending a lot of time as a volunteer at the animal shelter."

Sean was curious. "What kind of animals do they have at the shelter? Aren't they mostly dogs and cats?"

"Yes," Mr. Shaw answered. "However, at the present time I'm helping to care for a coatimundi. It was brought to the shelter by a woman who liked it when it was a cute baby animal, but doesn't want it now that it's an adult and has sharp teeth and bites. The woman claimed it was a gift from a friend who moved away, but between you and me, I'm sure the woman was lying. I think the coatimundi was taken from the wild in South America, smuggled into this country, and sold as a pet."

Mr. Shaw's cheeks and nose tuned red, and his eyes sparked with anger as he went on. "I can't understand the stupidity of smuggling wild animals out of their natural habitat and trying to make domestic pets out of them!"

A gray-haired woman opened the back door.

"Arthur!" she called.

"A wild animal has wild instincts, and can—"

"Arthur!" the woman persisted. "Mrs. Jones is here."

Mr. Shaw seemed to suddenly realize that his wife was calling him. He blinked a few times and said, "Yes, Agnes?"

"Mrs. Jones from the animal shelter is here," Mrs. Shaw repeated. "She's brought us the miniature dachshund you said you'd take care of while his owner is in the hospital."

Mr. Shaw beamed. "Of course, of course," he said. "Tell Mrs. Jones I'll be right with her."

He chuckled as he glanced at the muddy paw prints on Alan's clothes. "I see you've had another tussle with Rusty. I believe I'll be taking care of Rusty in another two weeks while

Mr. Everitt is traveling out of the county."

After Mr. Shaw left, Brian said, "He really likes animals. I bet he knows a lot about them—more than he let on."

Sean threw Brian a quick glance. "You think he knows what animal made this track, don't you?"

"C'mon, Sean," Alan said. "I heard everything that Mr. Shaw said. He didn't tell us anything to make Brian think that."

"Private detectives listen to what people *don't* say, as well as what they do say," Brian told Alan. "Sometimes what they don't say is important."

"Huh? I don't get it," Alan said.

"I asked Mr. Shaw a couple of direct questions," Brian said. "He didn't answer them. He just asked another question or talked more about animals."

Brian suddenly shoved the stack of plaster casts into Sean's hands and began to fish in the pocket of this jeans. "Here, Sean," he said. "You hold these. I think we've gone past just trying to identify an animal. We could be in middle of a mystery—one that needs the Casebusters to solve it. I'd better start taking notes."

But Brian dropped his pencil as a loud, high-pitched yowl made them all jump.

B RIAN AND ALAN raced between the house toward the direction of the noise.

Sean, carefully hanging on to the plaster casts, ran after them. He arrived just in time to see someone in the Webbers' driveway loading the last of a group of boxes into a van. A striped, furry paw reached out of one of the airholes in the sides of the last box, scratching furiously at the box as it tried to get out. The animal yowled again, its high screech wriggling up Sean's backbone, making him shiver.

"What's that?" he asked, moving closer to the van.

The man quickly shut the van doors and turned to face Sean. "Hi," he said. "Who are you?"

Alan stepped up and introduced Brian and Sean. "This is Mr. Webber," he said. "Brian and Sean are spending the weekend with us."

"I'd stay and get better acquainted, but I have to take my cats to the vet for their shots," Mr. Webber said.

"I never heard a cat make such a loud noise," Sean blurted out.

Mr. Webber just smiled. "He is noisy, isn't he?"

Brian reached for one of the plaster casts and handed it to Mr. Webber. "Do you have time to answer one question? We took casts of these paw prints in the woods, right outside the backyards, and we don't know what the animal is. Do you?"

At first Mr. Webber didn't answer. He looked surprised at the paw print. Then he frowned at it. Sean, trying to be helpful, said, "It looks sort of like a bear's paw, doesn't it?"

"It does," Mr. Webber said. "A lot like a bear. If a bear is wandering around in the woods, then you kids better stay out of there."

"Yikes!" Sean said.

Alan spoke up. "My mom and dad said there aren't bears in the woods anymore."

Mr. Webber looked at Sean. "I wouldn't be so sure," he said. "I heard that a few years ago a man hiked back into the woods, looking for bears, and he never came out and was never seen again." He leaned closer to Sean. "Word was that he came across an angry, hungry grizzly bear."

Scared, Sean took a step backward.

Brian flipped a page over in his notebook and began to write. "Do you remember the date the man disappeared? Or his name?"

Mr. Webber looked at Brian's notebook and scowled. "What is this, a quiz?" he asked.

"I'm just collecting information," Brian told him.

"I can't give you any. I told you, I've got to get my cats to the vet. I haven't got time to play games." Mr. Webber swung up into the driver's seat and slammed the door shut behind him.

With a screech of his tires, he backed his van down the driveway into the circular drive. But his van stopped short. A large truck, with a bright furniture company logo painted on the side, had just arrived, blocking the entrance to the road.

"That house on the other side of ours belongs to Cecelia Crane," Alan said. "She's a furniture designer who works from her home. She lives there with her elderly mother and aunt. Every once in a while the truck from the store comes by to load or unload pieces of furniture. While they're doing it, the road's blocked for a few minutes, but so far no one's complained."

Sean pointed to Mr. Webber, who was leaning out the window of his van, yelling at a pair of moving men, who were carrying a table from the van into Miss Crane's house. "Mr. Webber's complaining," Sean said.

"Does the furniture delivery truck come by often?" Brian asked Alan.

"Once every week or so," Alan said, and Brian made a note.

"What does the furniture truck have to do with the animal we're trying to track?" Alan asked.

"Maybe nothing. Maybe a lot," Brian said. "Investigators collect information. Then they sort through it to see what fits and what doesn't."

Alan began to laugh. "Where are you going to fit a furniture truck?"

Just then Alan's sister, Lucy, popped out of the Nashes' front door. "There you are!" she shouted. "I've been looking all over for you! Hurry up! You're late for dinner!"

With great sighs she led them to the kitchen and handed them paper plates.

Alan groaned as he looked at the table.

"Hot dogs and canned fruit cocktail. Don't tell me. It was your turn to cook tonight, wasn't it?"

Lucy sniffed. "Just be glad you're getting anything."

"Where are Mom and Dad?"

"They're putting up bookshelves. They thought they'd be through by this time, but it's taking a lot longer, so they said to go ahead and eat."

Sean was hungry. He began slathering mustard on his hot dog.

"Take your plates outside to the patio table, so you won't get the kitchen dirty," Lucy ordered.

Sean didn't mind. It was a beautiful evening. The sun was slowly setting, and the first star had come out. Sean listened carefully for any animal sounds besides the cricket chirps, but the woods were silent. He opened his mouth wide to take the first bite of his hot dog, when a loud scream ripped through the air.

5

A WOMAN DASHED across her backyard, between her house and the Nashes' house, and out to the street. Brian, Sean, and Alan ran after her. At the same time, Mr. and Mrs. Nash rushed out the front door of their house.

"What happened, Cecelia?" Mrs. Nash cried.

Miss Crane breathed heavily and leaned on Mrs. Nash's shoulder. "I'm sorry, Gloria," she gasped. "I didn't mean to scream. For a moment I was badly frightened."

"By what?" Sean asked. He saw that Brian's

notebook was out and ready.

"I was taking down my hummingbird feeder to refill it, when I came face-to-face with a very large raccoon," Miss Crane said. "That is, I think it was a raccoon, although it didn't have that dark mask around its eyes. The raccoon bared its teeth, as though it wanted to bite me, and then it hissed at me. I screamed because it frightened me. I've never heard a raccoon hiss!"

Mrs. Nash patted Miss Crane's shoulder. "There, there," she said. "It didn't hurt you. It's probably already run back into the forest."

"Miss Crane," Brian said, "my name is Brian Quinn, and this is my brother, Sean. If you don't mind I'd like to ask you a few questions. Do you have pets?"

"No," she said. "I don't have time for a pet, but I do like to watch the birds."

"Do you know much about raccoons?"

"I know nothing about them at all. I suppose that's why the raccoon took me by surprise." She ducked her head and smiled sheepishly. "I feel so foolish for screaming and running away from a raccoon."

"The animal you saw might not be a raccoon," Brian said. "Do you remember what kind of feet it had?"

"Ummm, yes," she said. "It had wide feet and long claws, and it hung onto the branch with its tail and back feet while it hissed and waved its front paws at me."

Brian and Sean looked at each other. Both of them were sure the animal hadn't been a raccoon. With wide feet and long claws, it had to be the mysterious animal they were tracking.

"Which way did it go?" Sean asked Miss Crane.

"I have no idea," she said. "I didn't stay around to find out."

Mr. Webber's van swung into the circular drive and straight into the Webbers' open garage. Although Mr. Webber passed the group on Miss Crane's front lawn, he didn't wave or even glance in their direction.

"Oh dear. I'm afraid Glen's angry with me," Miss Crane said. "The truck from the furniture store is here only a few minutes at a time, but today it blocked the road just as Glen wanted to get out." She sighed. "The men who brought my accent table did hurry, so Glen wasn't delayed long." She nervously ran her fingers through her hair.

"Why don't you come into the house for a

cup of tea, Cecelia," Mrs. Nash said. "You're still upset. You need to relax. Tell me about your table. What designs are you going to paint on it?"

Alan nudged Brian and Sean. "Let's go back to the patio and finish our dinner."

They cut between the houses and headed for the patio. But when they got there Alan stopped and said, "Oh, no! Look at the mess!"

The paper plates were lying on the ground. The hot dogs and buns hadn't been taken, but every scrap of fruit salad had disappeared.

"Rusty!" Alan complained.

"Not Rusty," Brian pointed out. "He would have eaten the hot dogs, but they're still here. Only the fruit salad is gone."

"Bears like sweet stuff to eat," Sean said. He glanced toward the woods and imagined he saw gleaming eyes staring back at him. His heart started pounding again.

"Bears would have eaten the hot dogs, too," Brian said. "Bears eat everything."

Sean gulped.

"Hey, look, Sean, it wasn't a bear," Brian said. "I think it was the mystery animal we're trying to find."

"I don't care about a mystery animal," Alan said. "I'm hungry, and I want my dinner."

Lucy glared at them suspiciously after Alan told her what had happened. "You're playing a trick on me. Right?" she asked. "A monster came through the woods and ate your fruit cocktail? C'mon. You can think up something better than that."

"Lucy, we're hungry!" Alan wailed.

"Well, okay," Lucy said. "But no more tricks.

They aren't funny."

She let them fill up their plates again, and they returned to the patio.

Much later, as they were going through Alan's video games, the doorbell rang. They could hear Mr. Webber's voice from the entry hall.

"No, thank you. No coffee. I can't stay. I came to ask you to keep the boys out of the woods. I'm concerned for their safety."

Mr. Nash said something they couldn't hear. Then Mr. Webber answered, irritation in his voice. "I realize that Alan knows his way around the woods near your home, but what if the boys stray a little farther than they should? I mean, there's been talk of bears . . ."

Finally, they heard Mr. Webber say, "Suit yourself."

The door opened and shut again, and in a few minutes Mr. Nash came into the room.

Alan quickly said, "Dad, we heard what Mr. Webber told you. He's wrong. Nothing's going to happen to us in the woods."

"I agree," Mr. Nash said. "He seems overly cautious. Maybe because he's never had children."

"He said something about bears," Sean said. He glanced at the darkness outside the window and shivered.

"I know," Mr. Nash said, "but he's wrong. There haven't been any bear sightings around here since—"

"Since the giant grizzly lived here." Sean finished the sentence.

Mrs. Nash joined them. "Mr. Everitt telephoned a few minutes ago. He seems to think the boys should stay out of the woods because they're endangering the animals who live there."

"What did you tell him?" Mr. Nash asked his wife.

"That the boys don't endanger the animals. They respect the animals. Making plaster casts of prints certainly won't bother them."

"What's the big deal with Mr. Webber and Mr. Everitt?" Alan asked. "Why are they acting so weird about our going exploring in the woods?"

"Who knows?" Mrs. Nash answered and sighed. "When we moved here I didn't think we'd have trouble with nosy neighbors." She looked at her watch and added, "Boys, it's late—way past your bedtime. Time for bed."

Without an argument, they started up the stairs. Outside the guest room door Alan said,

"We'll get up real early and eat breakfast. Then we can visit the giant grizzly bear's den."

"Cool," Brian said.

But Sean climbed into bed, dreading the next morning so much that he couldn't fall asleep.

Soon Brian's steady breathing came from the next bed, so Sean knew his brother was sleeping soundly. Sean rolled over and pushed his pillow into place for the umpteenth time. He glanced at the bedroom window.

There, staring in at him, was an animal face. The animal had rounded ears and a pointed snout like a bear, but it was smaller, with big eyes like a bear cub has.

"Yikes!" Sean yelled and jumped out of bed. "Bri! Wake up!"

Brian groaned and rolled over, so Sean sat

on him, trying to pull the quilt away from his face.

"What's the matter?" Brian managed to ask. He struggled and tried to dump Sean on the floor.

"Wake up and look!" Sean yelled in his ear. "We're on the second floor! Right? Well, there's an animal out there looking in the window!"

6

THE ANIMAL, startled, scrabbled across the ledge outside the window and disappeared.

Brian sat up and squinted at his wristwatch. "Calm down, Sean. Keep quiet. Do you want to wake everybody up?"

"But the animal . . ."

"It's almost midnight. Everyone else is asleep."

"Listen to me, Bri! Pay attention. I saw the animal we're trying to track."

Brian, fully awake now, climbed out of

bed. "Where?"

"He's gone. You missed him."

Brian found his notebook and pencil and turned on a lamp. "Okay," he said. "What was it?"

"I don't know."

"Haven't you ever seen an animal like it? Not even in a photograph or a drawing?"

"No. Never."

"Then describe it."

"It had a bear face and buggy eyes."

"Buggy eyes?"

"Yeah. And funny ears."

"Buggy eyes and funny ears? What kind of description is that?"

"A good description."

"Try describing the animal a different way," Brian said. "You said his face was like a bear's. Go on from there."

"Okay. It was like a bear's because it had a pointed nose, and I think it was furry."

"What were its ears like?"

Sean thought a moment. "Round. Like a bear cub's. Okay?"

"Tell me about his eyes."

"Bugg—uh—big and round."

"Bulging eyes."

"That's what I said."

"How large was the animal?"

Sean had to think about it again. "Ummm, not as big as Rusty, but lots bigger and longer than a raccoon."

"Any chance it could be Mr. Shaw's coatimundi?"

"No. I know what a coatimundi looks like."

Brian pulled on his jeans. "Could you

recognize the animal if you saw a picture of it?" he asked.

"I think so," Sean said.

"Then come with me, and be quiet. We're going to wake up Alan."

Alan just mumbled to himself as Brian tried to wake him, but when Brian said, "Sean saw the mystery animal," Alan sat up and stared.

"Where?" he asked.

"On the ledge outside our bedroom window," Brian said.

"What was it?"

"Sean isn't sure, so we need to use your computer encyclopedia. Okay?"

"Sure," Alan said. He hopped out of bed. "We'll have to be real quiet and not wake my parents," he said.

They tiptoed down the stairs, wincing when

the wood creaked, and made their way to the den, where they turned on only a small desk lamp.

Alan booted up the computer and inserted the CD-ROM encyclopedia. "What'll I look for?" he asked.

"Bears," Sean said quickly.

Brian shrugged. "Sean said it had the snout of a bear and ears like a cub. Maybe something will turn up."

They went through many types of bears—grizzly, Kodiak, brown bear, black bear, even koala, but at each photograph Sean shook his head.

"I don't know where else to look," Alan said. He turned off the computer. "We can work on it in the morning. Right now I'm sleepy. I'd like to get back to bed. C'mon."

As they reached the entry hall they stopped, startled by a strange, scratching noise outside the front door.

"Is something trying to get in?" Sean whispered, his voice trembling.

Alan gulped loudly. He snatched an umbrella out of a rack near the door and held it like a baseball bat. "It might attack us. We've got to protect ourselves."

Brian shook his head. "That's a strong front door, and it's locked. The animal won't be able to get in."

At that moment the door flew open.

Alan, Sean, and Brian yelled at the top of their lungs.

Lucy, who stood in the doorway, screamed.

Mr. and Mrs. Nash came running, and everyone began talking at once. Finally, Mr.

Nash shouted for quiet.

"But Dad, I just got back from baby-sitting, and . . . ," Lucy began.

Alan interrupted. "We didn't know Lucy was out baby-sitting. We thought she was the animal we were tracking."

"Ha! Tracking an animal at the front door? You expect anyone to believe that?" Lucy shouted.

"We were looking it up on the computer," Alan explained. "We were trying to see if Sean could recognize the animal's picture since he saw it."

"You were supposed to be in bed, not using the computer," Mrs. Nash said.

But Mr. Nash said, "Wait a minute. What animal did Sean see?"

"A bear," Sean answered.

"Just where did you see this bear?"

"He was looking in our bedroom window."

"When?"

"Just a little while ago."

Mr. and Mrs. Nash looked at each other. Then Mrs. Nash put an arm around Sean's shoulders. "You had a nightmare, dear," she said. "Too much excitement and too many sweets, I'm afraid. Now the nightmare's all gone, so go back to bed and back to sleep."

"But I wasn't asleep. I saw a bear. A real bear," Sean said.

Lucy glared at Sean. "You didn't see a bear, and you didn't have a nightmare," she said. "Also, I don't believe all that stuff about bears and the computer. The three of you were trying to play another rotten trick on me."

"No we weren't," Sean protested.

But Lucy scowled. "No more tricks. Understand? Or—just like I said—you're going to find yourselves in big trouble."

IN SPITE OF THEIR interrupted sleep, the early sunlight woke Brian, and he woke Sean. Alan was already down in the kitchen, getting out cereal and milk for breakfast.

"I tested the flashlights," Alan said and pointed to where they lay on the kitchen counter. "Hurry up and eat, and we can get going."

Brian quickly gobbled down his breakfast. "Wait till I mix up some plaster of paris."

But Sean ate more slowly. Mr. Everitt, Mr. Shaw, and Mr. Webber had warned them against going into the forest. Was it because they knew something and weren't telling?

"Hurry up, Sean!" Brian said. "We're ready to go."

Sean pushed back his bowl, still half-full of cereal. He wiped his mouth on his shirt, and picked up his flashlight.

Alan was familiar with the trail that led deeper into the woods, so their only stops were to pour plaster into the tracks made by animals Brian recognized. "Deer!" he said. "And over there—fox. I know those."

"I don't see any more of those wide foot-pads with claws," Alan told him.

"I don't either," Brian said. "I've been wondering about that. The animal's wild, not somebody's pet, so why is it hanging around the houses?"

"And our bedroom window?" Sean said.

"If you're through with that cast," Alan said to Brian, "let's get going. The grizzly's den is still about fifteen minutes away."

The forest was silent when they reached a small clearing. Alan pointed to the rock-face in the hill ahead of them, with an opening in it just wide enough for a large, fat bear to squeeze through.

Alan climbed inside the den first, and Brian soon followed.

For a moment Sean waited outside the opening, unwilling to crawl through it. He looked around at the lonely forest that surrounded him—the totally quiet forest. He couldn't hear a single rustle of leaves. Not even the small sounds of insects moving through the grasses. He listened carefully, but there wasn't even the trill of a bird to break the silence.

What if something came crashing through the underbrush? What if something rose up ahead of him, roaring loudly? What if it swooped down from the sky, claws gleaming, and he was outside, all by himself?

Sean bent down and scrambled through the opening into the cave.

"Phew!" he said and held his nose. "This place stinks!"

"Do any other animals use this den?" Brian asked.

"I don't think so," Alan said, but he quickly glanced into the darkness at the back of the cave. The beam from his flashlight would go only so far.

Sean gave a start. "What was that noise?" he asked.

"What noise?" Brian said.

"It was a kind of snuffle."

They all began edging toward the opening of the cave, but a louder, thumping noise stopped them.

"Wait!" Brian whispered. "Whatever made that snuffling noise isn't inside the cave. It's right outside the opening."

"Is it coming in after us?" Sean grabbed Brian's arm.

"What should we do?" Alan asked.

Brian didn't have time to answer. With a dull thump, something closed off the entrance to the cave.

Three flashlights snapped on. "Bri!" Sean gasped. "Someone shut us in here!"

8

I BET IT WAS Lucy," Alan said. "She's getting even with us."

Brian shook his head. "I don't think it's Lucy. Remember? Yesterday your mom said something about going shopping today with Lucy."

Alan's voice shook. "Then what closed off the cave? What if it's a rock? We can't move a big rock! How are we ever going to get out?"

"Help!" Sean yelled. His heart began beating hard.

"Calm down," Brian said. "It won't do any

good to panic." He crawled to where the opening of the cave was and stretched out his arm. Then he winced as his fingers touched the object. "Yuck!" he said. Whatever's there is warm and furry."

"I knew it! Bears!" Sean yelped.

"Try *Rusty*," Brian said. He shone his light on the opening, and they could see the white-and-brown splotches.

Brian pushed hard against Rusty, but the dog didn't move.

Alan and Sean squeezed in next to Brian at the cave's entrance. "Go away, Rusty!" Sean yelled and helped push at the dog's furry back.

"I bet somebody told Rusty to sit and stay," Alan said. "He's just obeying commands."

"Why would anyone tell him to sit at the cave's opening?" Sean asked.

"We've been warned not to go into the woods," Brian told him. "We didn't pay attention to the warning, so now someone is trying to scare us away."

"Why? It doesn't make sense," Alan said.

"We'll figure that out later," Brian said. "Right now, let's see if we can get Rusty to move."

He and Alan poked and prodded Rusty. They shouted his name, but nothing they tried did any good.

Then Alan said, "I wish we had some dog yummies to give him."

Rusty gave a wiggle, and they could hear his tail thump.

"Dog yummies!" Sean yelled.

At the magic words, Rusty jumped away from the opening to the cave, wiggling and barking. Sean, Alan, and Brian squirmed through the opening.

Sean looked through his pockets and found a crumbled oatmeal cookie for Rusty while Brian examined the forest around them. There was no sign that anyone had been there with Rusty, yet Brian knew that Rusty hadn't followed them. What if Rusty had come with someone and had obeyed that person's commands?

"Bri," Sean said, "who tried to scare us? We've got to solve this case."

"We will," Brian said. "But this time we're going to work the way Dad does. We're going to solve our mystery with the help of a computer."

He snapped his fingers at Rusty. "Let's go back," he said. "We haven't got much time

untitled

left, so we need to get to work."

As he turned on Alan's computer, Brian said, "The animal we're tracking isn't from around here. None of us have ever seen tracks like that before."

"If it isn't from around here, then how did it get here?" Sean asked.

"Remember what Mr. Shaw told us about people who illegally smuggle wild animals into the United States and sell them? He talked about a coatimundi. Let's look one up and see if that's the animal Sean saw last night."

Eagerly, Brian and Alan stared at the photo that came up on the computer screen, but Sean shook his head. "I told you it wasn't a coatimundi," he said.

"Okay. Let's try this another way," Brian told him. "Let's list all the things we know about the animal. It comes out at night. It eats fruit and has wide feet with long claws for climbing trees. It has a tail that can anchor it to a branch, and it has a face and ears like a bear."

He typed all the facts into the computer, then waited. Slowly, a photograph began to form. As it finally turned into a complete picture, Sean sighed with relief. "A kinkajou!" he cried out. "Wow! That's it!"

Brian read the text aloud. "It's sometimes called a honey bear," he said. "Sean, you weren't so wrong when you said it was a bear."

Alan read over Brian's shoulder. "The kinkajou has a prehensile tail and soft woolly brown fur. It's nocturnal and feeds on fruit, insects, and small mammals."

"Then why didn't it eat our hot dogs, too?" Sean asked.

"Hot dogs are *not* small mammals," Alan said.

Sean thought a moment, then made a face. "Yuck!" he said.

"Listen to this," Brian said and read aloud, "'Kinkajous live in tropical forests from Mexico to Brazil.'" He leaned back and looked at Sean and Alan. "That means someone must have brought it into the country or have bought it for a pet—someone in this neighborhood. We need to find out which of the neighbors traveled to Central or South America recently."

Alan frowned as he thought. "I'll give you information about the neighbors," he said.

"Wait!" Brian told him. He pulled out his notebook and pencil then nodded. "Okay. Go ahead."

"Mr. Everitt travels a lot," Alan said. "Last

week he left Rusty with Mr. Shaw, who said something about taking care of Rusty again in another week or so."

Brian checked through his notes, then nodded. "Go ahead. What about Mr. Shaw."

"I fed Mr. Shaw's pets the week before last when he said he had to go to Sacramento for a program about funding animal shelters."

"Don't forget Mr. Webber," Sean said.

"I was just getting to him," Alan said. "Mr. Webber was gone again last week on some kind of business, but his wife stayed home and fed their animals. She always does."

"We can leave out Miss Crane," Sean said. "She doesn't have pets."

"That's what she told us," Brian said. "But remember, every week or so trucks from the furniture company come and go from her house. She could be in the middle of an animal smuggling deal."

"How do we get one of them to admit they traveled to Central or South America for animals?" Alan asked.

"Nobody's going to admit it. Nobody's going to confess," Brian said.

"Then how do we find the one who's guilty?"

Brian and Sean looked at each other and smiled. Sean knew they were thinking the same thing. "We capture the kinkajou," Sean said.

"Then we might find out who's guilty when the smuggler tries to get him back," Brian said.

"Course, he might be hard to capture," Sean admitted.

Brian asked, "Sean, did you bring your camera—the one that takes night pictures without a flash?"

"Yes," Sean said and grinned. "Hey! Maybe we can at least get the kinkajou's picture!"

Brian grinned back. They were going to solve this case. He knew they would. "Okay," he said. "Now it's time to make some plans."

9

IMPATIENT BECAUSE they had to wait at least until dusk to carry out their plans, Brian, Sean, and Alan kept busy with other things. By early evening Brian had laid out his cleaned and labeled plaster casts on Alan's bed and called Mr. Nash to take a look at them.

"Very nice," Mr. Nash said. He picked up one of the kinkajou's prints. "So this is our mystery animal."

"Not a mystery anymore, Dad," Alan said. "We found out it's the paw print of a kinkajou."

"A kinkajou? In northern California?"

Alan's bedroom door flew open, and Lucy stormed in.

"Dad!" she wailed. "Make them stop!"

"Stop what?" Mr. Nash asked.

"Throwing pinecones at me!" Lucy said. "I was out in the backyard, minding my own business, when they started throwing pinecones."

"No, we didn't," Sean said. "We were up here, working on Brian's casts."

"Oh, sure," Lucy said.

"The boys are right," Mr. Nash said. "I've been here with them."

"Were you with them ten minutes ago?"

"Well, no, but . . ."

"Ha!" Lucy shouted. She went to the window and pointed. "I was right there under that tree, when they started throwing pinecones. Three of them even hit me! I bet they threw them from right up here!"

"We wouldn't have thrown pinecones," Alan said. "We would have thrown mushy, rotting banana skins, or dead frogs, or . . ."

"That's enough," Mr. Nash said. "Lucy . . . Alan . . . I expect you to get along with each other."

"Little brothers are a pain!" Lucy said and stomped out of the room. Mr. Nash followed her.

"Who threw the pinecones at Lucy?" Sean asked. "The kinkajou?"

"Sure," Brian said.

"I knew I liked that animal," Alan said.

"Look, it's just about dark," Brian told Sean and Alan. "Thanks to Lucy we know what tree the kinkajou must be hiding in. Let's carry out our plan."

Alan cut up some chunks of oranges, bananas, and apples. He put them into a plastic dish and carried it out to the backyard.

"Put it close to that tree," Brian whispered and pointed.

He and Sean, who had his camera ready to go, hid in the nearby bushes. Alan joined them.

In the moonlight they could see a long, thin animal crawl out of a hollow in the tree. It climbed head first down the trunk, its claws gripping the bark. Its tail, which was longer than its body, curled around a branch for support. Occasionally it stopped and raised its head cautiously. It had the face of a small bear cub, with the same rounded ears.

With its back feet still clinging to the tree

trunk, it reached out with its front paws and grabbed a piece of fruit.

Sean was so fascinated by what the kinkajou was doing, he almost forgot about his camera. But Brian poked him, and Sean took four photographs in quick succession.

Even though Sean stayed scrunched down in the bushes and tried to be very quiet, the kinkajou heard him. It stopped eating and looked around suspiciously. It hissed angrily at being interrupted before it scrambled up the trunk.

Just before the kinkajou disappeared into its hiding place there was the sound of running footsteps, and the beam from a flashlight shone on the kinkajou.

Someone in a sweatsuit, tennis shoes, and a cloth hat ran up to the tree. The person stopped, looking up at the hollow where the kinkajou was hiding. He pulled out a cloth bag and broke a long, thin branch from the tree. Then he pushed one end of the branch into the hollow, grunting and jabbing, trying to get the kinkajou to climb into the bag. The frightened kinkajou hissed frantically.

It was too dark to recognize the person at the tree, but Sean stood up and snapped two pictures.

Startled by Sean's movement, the person stepped backward into the dish of fruit and almost lost his balance.

The person spotted Sean and started for him, waving the stick, but Brian leaped up and shouted, "Stop!"

Confused, the person hesitated.

Alan raced into his house, yelling, "Mom, Dad!"

"Help me get him, Sean!" Brian cried out, as the person dashed into the forest.

Sean ran after him, but collided with Brian. They went down in a heap. When they managed to get to their feet the person had gone.

"Where's Alan?" Sean shouted. Panicked, he ran between the houses, heading for the street. Brian dashed after him. "Alan! Where are you?" Sean yelled.

In less than a minute, Alan came flying through the front door of his house shouting, "Dad's coming!"

Mr. and Mrs. Nash were right behind him.

Rusty, excited by the commotion, burst through the Everitts' open door, with Mr. Everitt—dog leash in hand—frantically chasing him.

"What's happening? What's the matter?"

Miss Crane called. She hurried to join the group. In what seemed like less than a minute Mr. and Mrs. Shaw and Mr. Webber showed up.

Brian groaned. There'd be no way to discover who the person in the yard had been by matching clothing to the person who'd gone after the kinkajou. All of the neighbors, with the exception of Mr. Webber, were wearing tennis shoes and sweatsuits. Miss Crane and Mr. Shaw wore cloth hats. Mr. Webber wore sweatpants, sandals, and a loud Hawaiian shirt.

Rusty bounced around the group, bumping into everyone, until Mr. Shaw quieted him with the words, "Sit, Rusty. Stay."

Sean nudged Brian. "It had to have been Mr. Shaw who made Rusty sit at the entrance to the cave, shutting us inside. He's the only one Rusty pays any attention to."

"Shutting you inside a cave? What's all this?" Mrs. Nash asked. She looked back and forth from Sean to Mr. Shaw.

Mr. Shaw sighed. "I'm sorry Rusty frightened you. I'd taken him for a walk, and he picked up your scent and followed your trail. I couldn't keep up with him. By the time I caught up, you were crawling out of the cave. Sitting in front of the cave entrance was Rusty's own idea. All I wanted to do was make sure you boys were safe. You hadn't listened to me when I warned you to stay out of the forest."

"Why did you want to keep us out of the forest?" Brian asked.

Surprised, Mr. Shaw said, "To protect you, of course. I suspected, after seeing that paw print in your plaster casts, that there was a wild animal loose in the area. I couldn't say anything until I knew more, but I didn't want you boys to get hurt."

"There *is* a wild animal loose," Brian told them. "It's a kinkajou."

"What in the world is a kinkajou?" Miss Crane asked.

"You saw it. It hissed at you," Sean told her.

"It's not only wild, it's out of its element. It lives in Central and South America," Brian explained.

"Then what is it doing here on Grizzly Hill?" Mrs. Nash asked.

"I think it was smuggled here," Brian answered.

"Smuggled? That's ridiculous!" Mr. Webber said.

"No, it isn't," Brian said. "We've been doing some investigating, and we believe that someone in this neighborhood is in the business of smuggling wild animals. This person probably had possession of the kinkajou until it escaped."

No one said a word. In shock, the neighbors looked at each other.

"You're just kids. What could you know about investigations and detecting?" Mr. Webber laughed.

"We're pretty good at solving crimes, Mr. Webber," Brian said. "And proving them. Sean and I can even prove that you're the animal smuggler."

"That's enough. You don't know what you're talking about," Mr. Webber snapped.

"Maybe they do," Miss Crane said. "I want to hear what Brian and Sean have to say."

Brian cleared his throat, thumbed through

his notebook, and began. "When Mr. Webber returned from his so-called errand of taking his cats to the vet for shots, he went into the house alone. His cats weren't with him."

"I left them at the vet's," Mr. Webber said.

"We can double-check," Brian told him. "But I don't think there's a vet involved. I don't think you were carrying cats."

"Of course they were cats! You even head them yowl."

"I heard something yowl, but I have a pretty good idea that you were carrying wild cats. Were they tiger cubs or bobcats?"

Mr. Webber's face turned red. "You can't prove anything," he insisted. "And I had nothing to do with that kinkajou. I'm not even wearing the same kind of clothes as the person who went after the kinkajou."

"If you weren't there, how do you know what kind of clothes the person was wearing?" Brian asked.

Sean pointed to Mr. Webber's shirt. "You must have put that on in a big hurry. It's buttoned up crooked."

As Mr. Webber grabbed at his shirt, Sean held up his camera. "I took pictures. They ought to prove something."

Mr. Webber gasped. He turned quickly and bolted toward his house.

10

RUN AFTER him!" Miss Crane shrieked. "Don't let him get away!"

"Wait!" Brian cried. "Do you hear that?" A long wail traveled up the hill, coming closer and closed.

"It's a siren!" Sean said. "Did somebody call the police?"

Lucy, her hands on her hips, stomped out of the Nashes' house and up to Brian, Sean, and Alan. "I am tired of your stupid pranks," she said. "And I am not going to put up with that horrible, hissing animal you put in our tree. I went out to the patio to get my sweater, and he threw something awful and squishy at me. You trained him to throw things at me, didn't you?"

"It's a kinkajou," Sean said. "He's a wild animal."

"And we didn't train him to throw things," Brian said. "You scared him, and he was trying to defend himself."

"Yeah," Alan said. "He took one look at you and probably started yelling, 'Save me! Save me!' "

"Very funny," Lucy said. "Well, I got even with you. For all I know your weird animal is rabid, so I called the sheriff."

"The sheriff! Just what we need!" Sean said.

As Mr. Webber ran from his house out to the van, the sheriff's car swung up into the circular drive. Pinned in the bright beams from the car's headlights, Mr. Webber threw his hands up before his eyes.

"I give up!" he yelled.

Lucy's mouth dropped open. When she was finally able to speak she said, "What's going on?"

"We'll tell you all about it later," Brian said. "In the meantime, thanks for helping the Casebusters wrap up another mystery."

JOAN LOWERY NIXON is a renowned writer of children's mysteries. She is the author of more than eighty books and the only four-time recipient of the prestigious Edgar Allan Poe Award for the best juvenile mystery of the year.

☾

"I was asked by Disney Adventures *magazine if I could write a short mystery. I decided to write about two young boys who help their father, a private investigator, solve crimes. These boys, Brian and Sean, are actually based on my grandchildren, who are the same ages as the characters. My first Casebusters story was a piece about a ghost that haunts an inn. This derives from a legendary Louisiana inn I visited which was allegedly haunted. Later, I learned the owner had made up the entire tale, and I used that angle in the story."*

— JOAN LOWERY NIXON